I'm So Blessed

Written by
CAIN

Illustrated by
Maja Andersen

B&H kids
Nashville TN

There once were siblings
who loved God and each other.
They wore feathers and sequins
and every bright color.

To sing along with the song in the book,
find "I'm So Blessed" by CAIN on your
favorite music streaming platform.

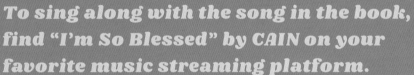

Text copyright © 2024 by CAIN
Art copyright © 2024 by B&H Publishing Group
Published by B&H Publishing Group
Brentwood, Tennessee
All rights reserved.
978-1-4300-9583-5
Dewey Decimal Classification: C152.4
Subject Heading: JOY AND SORROW /
HAPPINESS / EMOTIONS
Printed in Shenzhen, China, February 2024
1 2 3 4 5 6 · 28 27 26 25 24

They were known around town
for the song that they'd sing
and the way they'd find joy
despite everything.

"I'm so blessed, I'm so blessed, Got this heartbeat in my chest.

No, it doesn't matter about the rest. If I got You, Lord, I'm so blessed!"

One day, Tay-Tay Tangerine woke with a grin.
This Tuesday was special! Where to begin?
She'd pick flowers to wear; she'd run then she'd skip,
and bake chocolate chip cookies for a sunny picnic!

Then **"crack!"**

There was thunder. The blue sky turned gray.
A storm would soon spoil her very best day.

With each drop of rain, Tay-Tay wanted to cry.
She curled up in a blanket and tried hard to hide.

But then, an
idea!

She got her jacket and boots and smiled a mile wide.

Then she flew through her yard like a huge slip 'n slide.

Tay-Tay had a fun Tuesday, though it seemed sad at first.
She was a child of God at her best and her worst.

Her God was still good whether sunshine or rain;
with her thankful heart she smiled and she sang,

"I'm so blessed, I'm so blessed,
Got this heartbeat in my chest.
No, it doesn't matter about the rest.
If I got You, Lord, I'm so blessed!"

Maddie Melon began her birthday with joy.
"Maybe someone will bring me a cake or new toy!"

But as time went on,
Maddie's birthday went rotten.
She wondered if all of her
friends had forgotten.

"It's my special day! How could they forget?"
Maddie felt all alone. She was mad and upset.

But just when she felt things would never get better,
she thought about Jesus: how He'd love her forever!

Maddie put on an apron, grabbed some sugar and flour,
and baked her own cake in less than an hour.
Then her siblings appeared and shouted, "Surprise!"
Maddie couldn't believe it; she had tears in her eyes.

They ate cake and danced
in her bright living room,
and they all sang along
to their powerful tune.

"You think I can do it?"
Logo yelled to the crowd.
He knew he could flip
and soar high as a cloud.

Logo Lemon was brave,
and he moved with great skill.
He saw that a trick
would give folks a thrill.

But that sunny day
didn't go as he'd planned.

He *flopped* on the flip
he just knew he would land.

The crowd's cheers turned to
laughs as they saw his mistake.
He was embarrassed;
His heart started to ache.

But Logo couldn't give up.
He'd try it again.
His terrible day
wasn't going to win.

He took a deep breath . . .
put a bend in his knees . . .
then he *flipped* through the air—
landed this time with ease!

Though his first flip had flopped,
he stood tall and proud,
and with a strong voice,
he sang for the crowd.

I'm so blessed,

Got this
heartbeat
in my chest.

I'm so blessed,

No, it doesn't matter about the rest

If I got You, Lord, I'm so blessed!

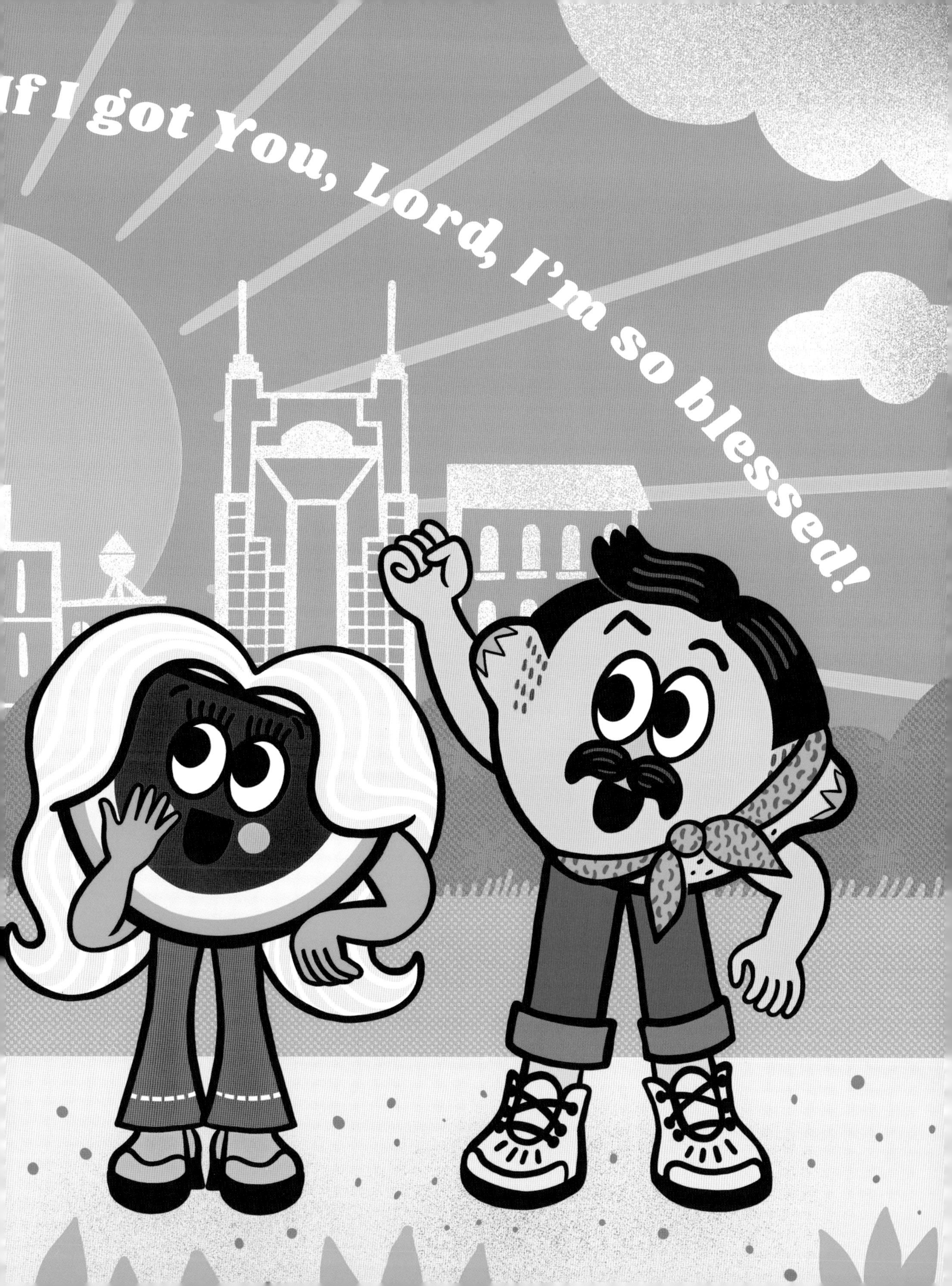

Through triumphs and trials,
God's kids can stand strong.
Because of His love,
to Him, they belong.

On all types of days, the good and the bad,
children of God can **always** be glad.

The world's biggest problems
won't disappear,
but, child of God,
the lesson is clear.
In every moment,
the worst or the best . . .

Sing it loud!
"I'm a child of God!
I'm so blessed!"